THE BIG WIN

by Kelli Chipponeri
illustrated by Dave Aikins

Ready-to-Read

Simon Spotlight/Nickelodeon
New York   London   Toronto   Sydney

Stephen Hillenburg

Based on the TV series *SpongeBob SquarePants*® created by Stephen Hillenburg as seen on Nickelodeon®

SIMON SPOTLIGHT
An imprint of Simon & Schuster Children's Publishing Division
1230 Avenue of the Americas, New York, New York 10020

4 6 8 10 9 7 5
Library of Congress Cataloging-in-Publication Data
Chipponeri, Kelli.
The big win / by Kelli Chipponeri. - 1st ed.
p. cm. - (Ready-to-read)
At head of title: SpongeBob SquarePants.
"Based on the TV series SpongeBob SquarePants created by Stephen Hillenburg as seen on Nickelodeon."
ISBN-13: 978-1-4169-4938-1   ISBN-10: 1-4169-4938-0
I. SpongeBob SquarePants (Television program) II. Title.
PZ7.C44513Big 2008   [E]-dc22   2007047086

The Bikini Bottom Relay Race
was just three days away. It only
happened once every five years!
SpongeBob and his friends
could not wait to compete.

It was the first day of practice. SpongeBob, Patrick, Sandy, Gary, Mr. Krabs, and Squidward were each going to compete in an event. "Team," said Squidward. "We have to train hard if we are going to win the golden booty treasure chest. So I am going to coach you!"

"Good idea!" said SpongeBob.
"Gold, sweet gold!" said Mr. Krabs.

SpongeBob practiced
ship-mast pole vaulting.
He ran, stuck the mast in the sand,
and swung himself over the ship.
"Great job, buddy!" said Sandy.
But Squidward was not impressed.

Then Patrick practiced
the sailing long jump.
He ran, flaring out his arms
and legs to jump far.
Jump farther!" called Squidward.

Sandy and Mr. Krabs practiced their
events. Mr. Krabs spun around,
then tossed the sand dollar discus.
Sandy ran and threw the javelin.
"Not good enough!" cried Squidward.
"What is it with you people!?"

Even Gary was going to compete!
He practiced hurdling coral.
We are never going to win if
you move this slowly, Gary!"
cried Squidward, annoyed.

Then it was Squidward's turn.
He picked up a kelp log
and practiced tossing it.
"Nice throw, Squidward!"
his teammates cheered.

Team meeting!" called Squidward.

The team jogged over happily.

Great practice!" cheered Sandy.

Am I sweaty?" SpongeBob asked.

Let's do it again!" cried Patrick.

Meow!" agreed Gary.

"Quiet!" said their coach.

"We will never win first place
  if we compete like that.
  Tomorrow we need to work harder!"

"Okay," said the team, unsure why.

They thought practice went well.
"We have to go for the gold!"
Squidward reminded them.
"Ah, sweet gold!" said Mr. Krabs.

The next day at practice
SpongeBob tried hard to vault high.
"HIGHER!" demanded Squidward.
"We must win that pirate's booty!"

...trick strained to make his arms
...d legs as long as possible.
...ONGER!" Squidward shouted.
...ink about the treasure chest!"

"Spin, Krabs!" cried Squidward.

"Throw it FARTHER, Sandy!"
barked Squidward. "Go for the gold!"

"Faster, Gary! FASTER!"
But Gary still moved too slowly.

Who am I kidding? We can't win.
I might as well just go home and
hang my head in shame,"
said Squidward, kicking the grass.

TWEET! Squidward blew his whistle.
"Okay people. My mother always says
if I want something done right,
I have to do it myself," he said.

I compete in all of the events,
e are sure to win! So, tomorrow
m going to practice them all!"
en he stormed off the field.

"Squidward wants to win so badly
that he is making us miserable,"
Sandy told the rest of the gang.

"Yeah. What's the point of being in the relay race if we do not have fun doing it?" asked SpongeBob.

The next day Squidward practiced all of his teammates' events.

When it was time for his event, Squidward was so tired he could barely throw the log.

"Squidward," Sandy said. "You can't compete in everything. You should trust that we will do our best."

"What if we do not win?" he asked.

"What, no gold?" cried Mr. Krabs.

Winning isn't everything," Sandy said.
Stop worrying about winning and enjoy
being teammates with us!"
Yeah!" agreed the group.
Not compete just to win?" he said.
Mmm, I guess we could try it."

The day of the race the team was
warming up, when *TWEET! TWEET!*
"Team meeting!" called Squidward.
The team huddled. "Just do
your best!" Squidward said.
"Go team!" they cheered.

y, SpongeBob, fly!"
eered Squidward.
mp, Patrick, jump!
hrow, Sandy, throw!"
ached Squidward.
in, Krabs baby, spin!"

27

"Hurdle, Gary, hurdle!"
cheered Squidward, as Gary
trailed behind the other hurdlers.

uidward picked up the
lp log and let it go.
e log flew through the air.
, Squidward!" cheered his team.

"Second place," sighed Squidward.
"True, we didn't win the gold,"
    said SpongeBob. "But we worked well
    together and had fun! We could have
    come in third."

course," replied Squidward,
you weren't such slugs,
could have won, but . . ."
UGS!" the team cried.
uidward smiled. "I mean slugs
the kindest way."

Squidward's teammates were right.
They did have a good time. And that
made them all feel like winners!